SPYING ON LIONS

NICK

ILLUSTRATE

📖 SCHOLASTIC

To Chris, my original Lucky brother

Scholastic Children's Books,
Commonwealth House, 1–19 New Oxford Street,
London WC1A 1NU, UK

A division of Scholastic Ltd
London – New York – Toronto – Sydney – Auckland
Mexico City – New Delhi – Hong Kong

Text copyright © Nick Arnold, 2003
Illustrations copyright © Jane Cope, 2003

ISBN 0 439 99426 8

Printed and bound in Great Britain
by Cox & Wyman Ltd, Reading, Berkshire
Cover lion image supplied by Powerstock

2 4 6 8 10 9 7 5 3 1

The right of Nick Arnold and Jane Cope to be identified as the
author and illustrator of this work has been asserted by them in accordance with the
Copyright, Designs and Patents Act, 1988.

CONTENTS

This advert changed my life.

Calling all teachers! Yes, that's me – Leo Dennis. To be exact, I'm a science teacher.

Are you tired of teaching? You bet!

I walked to school, thinking about the advert every step of the way. My car had broken down and, of course, it was raining. Cold water trickled down my neck and plopped onto my bald patch and ran down my glasses until I couldn't see where I was heading.

But I didn't notice. I was too busy dreaming of wide plains under blue African skies and endless hot days. I imagined huge honey-coloured lions with amber eyes watching me watching them.

Just then, a mean motorist splashed through a pond-sized puddle and the watery wave washed over me. The dirty, icy water soaked me from head to toe and everything in between, and I sploshed into school, dripping miserably. What's left of my hair stuck up in spikes and my socks made sad squelching sounds.

As luck would have it I wasn't teaching for the first lesson so I sneaked onto the stage of the school hall. It's a warm, snug place, hidden behind the heavy stage curtains. Soon my clothes were steaming on the radiator and I was sitting happily reading my newspaper in my underpants. I must have dozed off, because the next thing I knew, the curtains were opening. And what do you think I saw?

The head teacher and the whole school were there for a special assembly – they even had the mayor with them! Four hundred mouths dropped open and 400 pairs of eyes stared in horror. Then someone giggled. And soon the whole school was rocking and rolling and crying with laughter ... at me!

Everyone, that is, except for the mayor, the head teacher and myself. I was cowering behind my newspaper making pathetic whimpering noises, the head teacher looked ready to explode, and the mayor had turned an unhealthy shade of purple...

At that very moment I made up my mind to reply to the advert. I would go to Africa and watch lions – and the sooner the better!

GETTING STARTED

December 25

I've just eaten my Christmas dinner. I'm feeling full to bursting – but I don't want to talk about my bulging tum. I'm dreaming of next year...

I just can't believe my luck. Wildwatch have given me the job! Early next year (that's really soon), I'm flying to Africa to watch lions! I'll be keeping a diary of everything I see, and Wildwatch are going to make it into a book. It's a dream come true...

You see, I'm really into lions. I've had a thing about them ever since I was a little kid. I can't remember how it all started, but I think it was bound to happen. My parents called me Leo because I was born in August under the sign of Leo the lion, and Leo actually means "Lion" in Latin.

My interest in lions grew into an interest in the whole of nature, which led me to study biology at college. Now I'm a science teacher at Summerhill School and I like to think I'm quite popular with my pupils. Here's what I look like today...

Well, there's no point in lying – I'm chubby and I wear glasses. Go on, have a laugh. I'm used to it – I *am* a teacher!

The thought of going to Africa is exciting. But I'm a bit scared, too. At my interview they told me the

THIS IS ME NOW!

kind of things to expect, and I nearly gave up the idea on the spot. For one thing I won't be staying in a luxury hotel – I'll be living in a tent.

HOME SWEET HOME

And then there's all those dangers I'll be facing. I went on a Wildwatch training day last month, and I've jotted down a few notes:

DANGERS IN AFRICA

1. Don't get lost at night - you might be attacked by a lion.
2. Remember to wear thick socks so blood-sucking ticks can't bite you.
3. Tip out your boots in the morning because a poisonous scorpion might be hiding in them.
4. Watch out for poisonous snakes hidden amongst rocks or long grass.
5. Never swim in lakes or rivers. You could be attacked by a hippo or eaten by a crocodile.

I also needed jabs against a frighteningly long list of diseases such as typhoid, a gut disease spread by dirty fingers. The injections hurt! The doctor tried to stick the needle in my arm, but he kept missing the vein and I ended up with the jabs stabbing my bottom!

Luckily I didn't need an injection for the most dangerous disease of all – malaria. This is spread by mosquitoes and causes fever and even death. I should be OK though, as long as I take anti-malaria pills each day.

Anyway, despite the dangers and the warnings, I'm still keen to go, and I'm about to start packing. Well, maybe I'll leave it until tomorrow. After all it *is* Christmas Day, and right now I think I've earned a slice of cake!

December 26

Another big meal and I'm full up – again. I've been pinned to the sofa for the last two hours by Ginger, my pet cat. Ginger likes to snooze on me and if he's disturbed he gets cross and attacks my trousers.

Anyway, Ginger has kindly agreed to move, so I can get up and write this diary. If only he could understand where I'm going. After all, I'll be spending time with his close relatives! I'm leaving him with my neighbour, Mrs Matthews. She's dotty about cats, so I'm sure he'll be well looked-after.

MRS MATTHEWS AND GINGER

Now to start packing. Wildwatch gave me a list of things to take, and last week I went shopping. Mind you, these are just the basics! I'll need to buy food, tea, coffee, water and other vital supplies in Africa.

LIST FOR AFRICA

Binoculars
Night glasses (to see in dark)
Digital camera with zoom lens and
waterproof case
Diary, notebook, pens and pencils
Compass and map
Writing paper and envelopes
Torch
Books about lions
Radio
Spare batteries for
torch and radio
Swiss army knife (including tin opener)
Camping stove, paraffin and lighter
Kettle, saucepan, mug, bowl,
knife, fork and spoon
50 packets of dried soup
mix (vegetable)
Sealed bug-proof food containers
Soap, razor and spare razor blades
Hand mirror, hairbrush, comb and shampoo
Toothbrush and 12 tubes of toothpaste
Plastic bowl
Cloths and washing-up liquid

First-aid kit, including water-sterilization tablets; sunblock; antiseptic; anti-malaria, diarrhoea and constipation pills; painkillers; bandages and scissors

Insect repellent (super-strength) and a fly swat

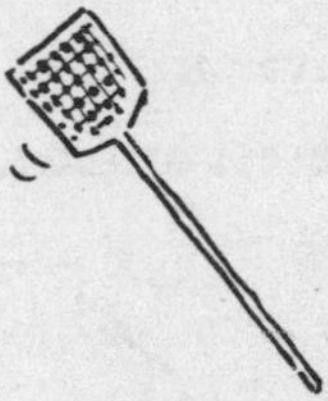

Tent, sleeping bag, mosquito net

Camp bed and inflatable pillow

Walking boots

Sunglasses

Umbrella

Waterproof coat

Waterproof tent bag

Toilet paper, bucket, trowel and disinfectant

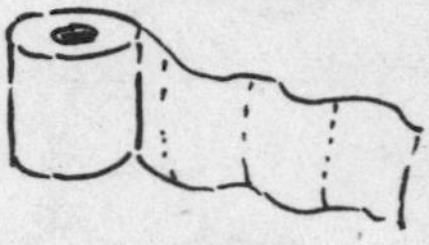

Rubbish bags

Large water bottle

Money belt for valuables and passport

Sticky tape and string

A few hours later

I've packed everything on the list. Now what have I forgotten?

Ah yes, clothes! I think I'll start on them tomorrow...

January 7

I can't believe I'm actually here! I'm sitting in my tent in the middle of Africa, and writing this diary! By the middle of Africa, I mean Lion Lodge Safari Camp. The Safari Camp is in the Masai Mara Game Reserve, 240 km west of Nairobi, the capital of Kenya, in East Africa. And if you're still not sure where I am, this map should help.

I AM HERE!

KENYA
NAIROBI
MASAI MARA
GAME RESERVE

Right now I'm feeling tired. But I'm excited too, and my brain is buzzing with everything that's happened since I arrived. I flew into Nairobi the day before yesterday. Getting off the plane was a shock to the system. I'd boarded the plane in a winter sleet storm, and left it on a warm damp tropical day in Nairobi. Well, straight away my glasses steamed up and I bumped into the man in front of me. We tumbled on top of two large ladies from a visiting gospel choir. What a start! I'm glad the security guards saw the funny side of it...

Still, at least I managed to buy a good hat in Nairobi. You really need a hat out here to protect your face from the hot sun. I think it makes me look rather dashing – don't you?

THAT HAT!

Sleeping in a tent takes some getting used to. It feels odd having nothing above your head, except for a mosquito net and tent fabric, and I've jotted down a few little "tent" grumbles.

DRAWBACKS OF SLEEPING IN A TENT

1. It was chilly last night and I had an annoying mosquito for company. Thank goodness for the mosquito net!

LITTLE PEST!

2. The animal night-life is noisy. Insects shrill and click, and damp places are full of croaking frogs. These pesky frogs are so loud you can't hear yourself speak.

ANTI-SOCIAL FROG!

3. My bed is hard, and this morning my poor back felt as stiff as a creaky old door.

15

Yes, you've guessed it, I didn't sleep too well!

I've spent most of today unpacking. You know what it's like arriving in a new place? If not, imagine starting a new school. I spent two hours trying to find everything ... now where did I put that Swiss Army knife?

A few hours later

The Masai Mara Game Reserve is near the border with Tanzania and it's really part of the Serengeti National Park to the south. The Masai Mara is one of the best places in the whole of Africa to see lions. Here's a map to show you the area close up:

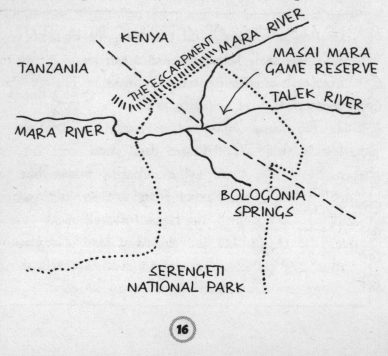

The Mara River coils like an oversized snake to the west, and near the river there are marshes and luggas (rivers that are mostly dry except in the rainy season). Across the river to the north-west there's a big slope called the escarpment, and there are hills to the east and north. The Masai Mara covers 1,672 square km – that's as big as the whole of London with room to spare.

Anyway, tomorrow I'm off to explore it.

January 8

Today Mr Edwards, the camp manager, drove me out to see the park. It was a hot, sticky day as we bumped along the dirt roads in the Land Rover. The grass is long and lush after what they call the "short rains" and there are pools and puddles everywhere you look. Mind you, if those are the short rains I hate to think what the long rains will be like! They're due in April.

After a couple of hours we reached the bottom of the escarpment. The first thing I saw were lots of boulders and thorny bushes where leopards like to lurk. (I didn't see any, worse luck!) But Mr Edwards said we should climb the slope for an amazing view over the plains. He led the way, but I was soon puffing and panting and could feel the sweat soaking through my itchy shirt.

We looked back and I reckoned the view was worth the climb. The plain stretched away into the hazy distance. It was mostly grass, but you could see thickets of silvery-grey croton bushes and a few acacia trees looking like a giant's umbrellas. It looked timeless, like nothing had changed for 10,000 years. Everything was so quiet, I felt I ought to whisper. You could almost

touch the silence, it seemed to fill the world, and all I could hear was the wind sighing in the spiky bushes.

I peered through my binoculars and spotted some baboons, zebra and antelope. Then I saw a giraffe looking like a crane on legs with its slender nodding neck. I couldn't see any lions but I knew they were out there ... somewhere.

LIFE ON THE PLAINS

Mr Edwards tells me there are over 550 lions in "the Mara" (as he calls the park), and there are about 22 prides (lion families). Once I've found a place in the Mara for my tent, I'll be looking for my very own lion cub to watch for this diary!

January 10

I've only just sorted out a site for my tent, and last night was my first away from the camp. What a terrible night it was! But I'll tell you the dreadful details later.

My tent is on an open plain, about five km from the Safari Camp – that's five km closer to where the lions live. I've got to take care living here and remember everything I learnt on my Wildwatch course. For example, I have to beware of tsetse flies – they look like this:

WINGS CLOSE
TO BODY

DARK GREY BODY
KILL ON SIGHT!

The flies suck blood and can spread a disease called "sleeping sickness". It causes fever and the urge to go to sleep, and (you might find this hard to believe), it makes you want to stuff meat in your mouth.

I've also got to keep out of the midday sun, or wear my sunblock and hat. Well, it's easy to forget, and my face and arms have already turned as red as a well-cooked lobster. They feel hot enough to glow in the dark!

I'm definitely missing the camp. I know I grumbled at the time, but it was luxury compared to here! Back at the camp there are toilets and showers and a shop. Now I have to use what I've brought with me. Last night I made a list of everything I'd be doing without while I'm here.

YOU CAN FORGET ABOUT...

Hot showers
Indoor toilets
Iced drinks
Cold beer
Ice cream with
chocolate bits on top
Hot buttered toast
Clean clothes
Nice cold milkshakes
(about 30 items left out here)
Conclusion: What am I doing here? I must be crazy!!!!!

Anyway, I was going to tell you why I didn't sleep last night.

Just as I finished my list, I heard a lion roar. It was a scary sound – like a burp, a growl and a howl mixed up, and it sounded very close. When I've seen lions in the past, they've always been behind bars. Now I don't like the thought of lions in cages, but at that moment I'd have been happy to be safely caged myself. And out here there are no barriers, no protection – it's like wobbling on a tightrope without a safety net.

My legs turned to shaky jelly.

So I tried to reason with myself. "Now, Leo," I said in a high squeaky scared voice, "the lions are a long way off. They're only keeping in touch with their pride and warning other lions to keep away."

Well, maybe. Being a science teacher I know that

WOBBLE! WOBBLE!

sound travels further at night, bouncing off layers of warm and cold air. That's why you can hear a lion roar EIGHT km away after dark.

I peered through my door flap and tried to work out where the sound was coming from. Then I remembered stories of lions padding around human camps and biting people's heads off. I decided to stay well inside the tent.

Then the roar came again.

It seemed louder and closer, and the sudden sound made me jump. But you can't jump too high in a tent. I smashed into the roof, which promptly fell down on my head. My glasses must have fallen off my nose because the next thing I remember was the CRUNCH as I trod on them. I'm glad I packed some sticky tape to mend them with!

I spent the next two hours putting my tent back up by the light of my torch. Then I lay still on my camp bed with my heart going WHUMP, WHUMP, WHUMP! I'm thinking about writing to Wildwatch – I wonder if they'll let me go home early?

LUCKY THE LION CUB

January 14

Lions roaring in the night, ha! A seasoned bush-camper like me isn't bothered by a few lions! Yes – I'm getting used to living here, and my sunburn is healing nicely, even if my peeling face does look like something out of a horror movie.

Mind you, there are so many things to remember. I have to beware of snakes – poisonous black mambas can lurk in the long grass. I have to bag up my rubbish so the smell won't attract hyenas or jackals. Each week the rubbish bag is collected by a driver from the Safari Camp, who brings me 50 litres of water. That's my water for the week and I mustn't waste a drop. I try to use my warm cooking water for washing and shaving – but it can be disgusting when there are bits of food floating about in it.

But back to the lions. Round here, lions roaring are as common as yowling cats back home. But lions hardly ever attack campers – so Mary says. I ought to tell you about Mary. She's been studying lions in the Mara for two years and she's going to be my guide whilst I'm writing this diary.

MARY

Mary is half Masai (they're the local tribe). She speaks Maa, the Masai language and she also speaks Swahili – the official language in Kenya. So all in all, Mary's a useful person for me to know.

Mary says a lioness she's been watching has given birth, and tomorrow we're off to find the cubs – there's a boy and two girls. So at long last I'll be seeing the lion cub who'll star in this diary – it's all very exciting. Er… I'd better stop writing now. A scorpion has just crept over my foot. OK, so a scorpion sting won't exactly kill me – I'll just be hopping around in agony holding a sore foot. But that's the kind of excitement I can do without…

I've actually seen a lion! It was an awesome experience, but let me tell you the whole story.

We set off before dawn in Mary's battered Land Rover, with the headlights on full beam. We had to leave early because it's a long journey and we wanted to get a full day watching the lions. Mary had an even earlier start because she lives in a bungalow outside the Mara and she came to pick me up.

The Land Rover is vital to carry our equipment, binoculars, cameras, radio, and other supplies, and you really do need a car to watch lions since a lion's territory (that's the area it hunts in) can be well over 200 square km.

SEE ANYTHING?

Six months ago Mary placed a radio transmitter collar on the mother lioness, and that makes our job easier, because if we can find her we can find her cubs.

It was cold and I was half asleep, but it was worth getting up early just to see the sunrise. The sun looked like a red-hot coal in a fire, and it lit the eastern sky with gold and crimson. The first streaks of sunlight touched the escarpment and slowly spread across the Mara, turning the plains orange with purple-blue shadows. We heard a distant lion roar and I made out a shadowy group of antelope standing stiffly to attention and staring in that direction.

The journey took two hours and one broken fan belt. Mary always carries spare parts, and she's a dab hand at repairs – unlike me. I don't know a gasket from a clutch cable! I did offer to help, but Mary said I was getting in the way, and after it got light I wasn't even needed to hold the torch.

So I sprawled in the shade, waving away the flies and listening to the birds singing and the insects chirruping in the grass. Once the sun came up the day became hot. My armpits were soaking, and big sweaty drops started rolling down my nose in an off-putting fashion.

Right now the Mara is like a bird holiday resort. Birds from other parts of the world fly in to get away from the winter in their own countries. I'm no expert, but with the help of Mary's wildlife book I spotted a cuckoo from India, a Caspian plover from Russia, and a stork from Spain. Then I saw swallows from Europe swooping for insects amongst the acacia trees.

CUCKOO

STORK

PLOVER

SWALLOW

Eventually Mary fixed the broken fan belt and I had to hold up something that looked like a TV aerial whilst Mary fiddled around with her radio receiver. She was trying to pick up signals from the lioness. We set off in the direction of the signals – once more jolting and bumping along the dirt tracks until my long-suffering backside was numb. At last we stopped. Mary touched my arm and pointed to a dead tree about 200 metres away – and there, lying quietly in the shade, was the lioness.

Wow! I thought. She was the first wild lion I'd ever seen and I stared through my binoculars, hardly daring to take my eyes off her. I was amazed by how big she was. I reckoned she weighed twice as much as me – and I'm no lightweight! Just one of her paws looked as big as my head! She could easily gobble me up for dinner and still have room for pudding. She was magnificent, but I couldn't help noticing that her nose was a little larger than other lions I'd seen.

WHAT A NOSE!

"Listen!" whispered Mary excitedly. "Can you hear the cubs calling?"

All I could hear was the wind in the grass, so I tried harder and could just make out a high throaty mewing.

"They're normally really quiet," said Mary. "But they know their mother is nearby. They're calling for milk and saying they're all right."

Five hundred years ago, people in Europe thought that all cubs were born dead and brought to life when the lioness breathes on them. Well, that's just a stupid old story, but you can see where the idea came from. The cubs really are helpless at this stage in their lives. Just like kittens, they can't see and they can't walk and they don't even have any teeth of their own.

Most lionesses are good mums. After being pregnant for 14–17 weeks the mother lioness will nurse her cubs every day for eight weeks. At night whilst they sleep, she goes hunting for food and her body uses the meat to produce milk for the cubs. She really needs to find food because the baby lions can want feeding 15 times a day and the lazy male lion doesn't bother to help at all!

IT'S WOMEN'S WORK!

Being a teacher I can't resist telling you some facts:

LEO'S LION NOTES
LIONS AND CATS

1. Lions belong to the same "family" (or "group" of animals) as cats, so it's not surprising that lion cubs and kittens have a lot in common.

2. Lions even purr just like cats. Mind you, lions don't purr as often as cats because they can only purr when they breathe out.

It's odd to think my cat Ginger is a relative of the lion. Is that why he's so fierce sometimes?

We visited the lioness three times this week without seeing the cubs. Mary says they're too young for us to risk disturbing them and I was put off by the sight of their mum on guard duty, anyway. But at least I've had a chance to see the territory where the lions live. It's mostly open plain, with some areas of bushes and a pond called a "water hole". Here and there you can see sticking-out rocks where the lions love to laze about in the sun.

Mary showed me how to look for lions on foot and I've jotted down her advice in my notebook:

WHEN LOOKING FOR LIONS...

1. Stand upright so the lions can see you – they'll feel more cross if they think you're sneaking up on them.

2. Don't make sounds or sudden movements that might upset them.

3. Don't get close to a lion. If you find yourself too close, slowly back away without showing fear.

4. Never look a lion in the eye. It makes the lion nervous and a scared lion is more likely to attack you.

You may be wondering if lions really are dangerous – I've been wondering that myself this week! The answer is well, maybe. Humans don't have as much meat on them as antelope or zebra, and because lions aren't used to eating humans they don't usually bother to hunt us.

You've got more chance of being attacked if you act scared.

I'm going to act real brave when there are lions around – I hope they'll be fooled!

January 28

The BIG NEWS this week is that I've finally seen the cubs! Here's how it happened: two days ago Mary and I were watching the lioness. I'm calling her Bignose (no prizes for guessing why).

It was a lovely bright morning and the clear blue sky was full of dazzling sunshine. As usual we had been watching Bignose through binoculars when suddenly she disappeared. Then Mary nudged me and pointed. Bignose was back and she had a little furry bundle in her mouth – a cub. She went back for another, and another – there were three cubs in all. It was as if the lioness mum was inviting us to drool over her cubs. My heart was pounding with excitement.

The cubs looked helpless, like tiny kittens, in the mighty jaws of the lioness. Their faces reminded me of kittens too, but they had bigger noses and smaller ears – and the cubs were all spotty like leopards! Mary told me that lion cubs have spots so that hyenas and other beasts can't see them too easily.

Hyenas are the big danger. Hyenas and lions HATE one another. For example, a lone hyena might be eaten by a lion, but one lion on its own could be ripped to bits by a gang of hyenas. If the hyenas find our lion cubs, they'll kill the lot. Chomp, chomp, b-u-r-p – not a very nice thought, so I'd better change the subject...

GRRR!

The cubs were dazzled by the sunshine because their eyes had just opened. All they did was toddle around making helpless little cries. Then one prodded his mum's tummy. Has a dribbling cat ever padded about on your lap? Kittens and lions prod their mum's tummies to make her give them milk, and adult cats do this to humans.

After their feed the cubs snuggled up to their mum, closed their eyes and went to sleep. One of the cubs has a bigger nose and whiter chin than the others. This cub had his chin on the others' backs and looked like he was smiling.

"That's the one I want to write about," I said.

"Are you sure?" Mary asked doubtfully.

"Well, at least I can tell him apart from the others."

"If there are no distinct markings, you can tell cubs apart by the pattern of their whiskers," said Mary. "Adult lions are easier because they nearly all have scars from being in fights. The males' manes are often different colours too – reddish, black, blond..."

"Like humans," I said.

Mary nodded.

"So what's wrong with having that cub for the diary?" I asked.

"He's the smallest," said Mary sadly. "The weak cubs often don't survive. This cub will be lucky if he lives one year."

Well, Leo Dennis is nothing if not stubborn, so I stuck to my guns. "Stupidity!" That's how some people describe it.

"Lucky, eh?" I replied. "Well, that's what we'll call him – and let's hope he is!"

THAT'S LUCKY STANDING ON BIGNOSE!

But since then I've been wondering: what would happen if I keep this diary and Lucky doesn't make it? Perhaps I ought to be writing about another cub?

February 4

Life won't be easy for Lucky. I've seen the cubs three times and I'm pleased to report that they're fine – including Lucky. But he's the smallest, weakest cub, "the runt of the litter," as the old saying goes. On Monday I saw the cubs feeding and the other cubs shoved Lucky aside. He mewed once and then wriggled back in amongst them. Well, at least he's got spirit!

This week we've been joined by James, Mary's 12-year-old son. Like me, James is really keen on lions and he knows an amazing amount of lion facts. James says he wants to be a scientist when he grows up and he enjoys listening to me talking about science. Yes — let that be a lesson to you, readers, some people are interested in their science lessons!

We had a great view of the cubs yesterday. Bignose winked at us sleepily and dozed and the cubs cuddled up to her. They all looked warm and snug and contented, but not for long...

LEO'S LION NOTES
SLEEPING LIONS

1. Lions never sleep for long, and even when they're asleep it's more of a snooze — not a zonked-out slumber like us humans.

2. Lions rest for up to 20 hours a day — compared to less than three hours for an elephant and roughly eight hours for a human.

3. Lions are not lazy. They can be very active, especially at night. A lion can trot eight hours non-stop in a night of hunting and cover over 40 km, so they really need all that rest.

It makes me tired just thinking about it!

After a few minutes, the lioness woke up, yawned and stretched. Lions always do this — have you ever seen a cat yawn and stretch? Try watching one and see what happens! I bet they'll dig in their front claws, stick their bottom in the air and stretch themselves — just like Bignose!

CAT STRETCHING

LION STRETCHING

Just then James spotted a group of buffalo. For Bignose it's a bit like seeing a month's supermarket shopping plodding up the garden path. A big buffalo could feed her for a week, but it's risky to attack one without the help of other lions. These creatures are like living tanks — they can run at 50 km an hour, their skin is 2.5 cm thick and they can smash into a lion with the force of a speeding car. Imagine being chased by a car with horns!

Suddenly the buffalo spotted Bignose and the cubs. The big male stopped and stared. Like all buffaloes he had a grumpy face with droopy lips. If anything he looked even more bad tempered as he

lowered his head with
its big arched horns.
He was making ready
to charge at any
moment. My mouth
went dry and I
wondered what would
happen to Lucky. I
could hardly bear to
watch.

MISERABLE BUFFALO!

Bignose stared at the buffalo and calmly stood up.
What a sensible mum – she sloped off into the long
grass and quietly led the cubs to another hideout!
Lucky was trotting in the rear. He didn't look at all
scared – but then he didn't understand the danger.

I love the way that lionesses walk. They slink like
a supermodel on a catwalk and I reckon they're the
queens of cool. Yes – I know what you're thinking:
"He's a teacher, what does he know?" But then you
haven't seen my ultra-cool dancing technique!

February 11

I'm feeling like a proud dad this week. On Monday
I saw Lucky yawn – and guess what? He's got his first
canine teeth (they're the teeth known as "fangs").
He'll grow another set in a year or so.

Lucky might be the smallest, weakest cub, but he's getting bigger every day and he and his sisters have begun to lose their spots. My little cub is growing up!

BRAND NEW FANGS!

Wednesday was the first time I saw Lucky and his sisters eating meat. Bignose emerged from the grass with a fly-blown strip of flesh in her mouth. I hate to think where it came from – probably a dead zebra – and it looked gross! It's like your mum feeding you disgusting titbits from the dustbin!

Mary and I were hiding behind rocks and watching through our binoculars. I was curious to see what Lucky and the cubs would make of the mouldy meat morsel. In fact they weren't too happy. Lucky drew back and I could see him thinking, "Urgh – what's this?" But, prompted by Bignose, the cubs sniffed the

meat and began to chew at it. Lucky was shouldered aside but he padded round the others until he found room. The cubs will need milk for at least five to six months – but from now on they'll eat meat whenever they get the chance.

Then Bignose licked the cubs with her rough pink tongue and Lucky climbed over the others to be the first in line. He might be the runt of the litter, but he's not going to let that stand in his way. Lions lick themselves after feeding because the blood attracts flies. Sometimes

YUK!

licked-up fur gets swallowed and forms nasty balls which get caught in their throats, so they nibble grass. It is thought the grass helps them sick up the fur balls. Er, sorry to be disgusting, readers! Nature ain't always nice.

I'm going to call Lucky's sisters Orange and Lemon because one has a slightly reddish coat and the other is more of a yellowish colour. Back at Summerhill School the kids say someone's a "lemon" if they're a stupid person, so I'm not sure if it's a polite name, but then lions don't understand English.

On Friday we watched Lucky, Orange and Lemon learning to hunt. The cubs were just playing, but their games are training them for when they're older and have to hunt for real.

Have you ever seen kittens play? Well, lion cubs are the same. They'll chase anything that moves, like a leaf blowing in the wind or an insect in the grass. They creep up and pounce on the target and they draw it in and bite it. As the smaller cub, Lucky has been a bit scared but he's taking part more and more. He loves playing these games and I love watching them. I could sit there for hours.

February 18

I'm still shaking and my fingers are tingling with fright. I'm writing this while I'm in shock and my head is reeling with what happened. Lucky has had a brush with death!

Mary and I were hiding behind a boulder, watching Lucky, Orange and Lemon playing on some rocks. Just then I spotted something slithering along the ground and my blood turned to ice.

It was a *snake* – a slippery POISONOUS snake!

Imagine a brown looping body with a mean ugly face and two scary staring eyes. I knew what sort of snake it was – I'd seen one on TV. It was a spitting cobra – and it gets its name because it spits deadly poison!

Lucky was closest to the snake. He stared at this curious creature in fascination and for an awful moment I thought he was going to do something stupid – like leaping on top of it.

I laid down my binoculars. I knew I had to rescue Lucky, but Mary grabbed my arm. She told me quietly that we were here to watch the lions, not to get involved. Besides, she reminded me, the cobra is just as dangerous to humans.

Praying that Lucky would be safe, I picked up my binoculars and watched. My fingers felt numb from gripping the sides so tightly. Just one tiny drop of poison in Lucky's eyes would blind him – and out here a blind lion cub has less chance than a cookie in a cookery class.

The snake gave an evil hiss and Lucky leaped back

with a little cry of surprise. I was startled too and gasped in shock. Two watery jets squirted from the snake's mouth like deadly water pistols.

BE CAREFUL, LUCKY!

Lucky's instincts had saved him, he heard the snake's hiss and he knew something was wrong. As the poison splattered on the rock, the snake reared up. Its body swayed as it aimed its head for a second deadly spit...

Suddenly Bignose appeared. With a growl, she sprang onto the rock and scooped Lucky up in her mouth. Lucky seemed more surprised by this than by the snake. But he went limp as cubs always do when carried. I gave a great gasp of relief. It was as if someone with a big smile had handed me a lovely present all wrapped up in rustling tissue paper.

February 25

This week Lucky made an exciting discovery, and got into trouble. Bignose and her cubs have taken to lying on a small rocky hill near the water hole. Apart from a few young acacia trees, there aren't too many plants, so the lions have a good view over the water hole and the wide green plains beyond.

The cubs were playing, but after a while Lucky lost interest in the game and decided to explore the water hole. He picked his way down the hill, jumping softly amongst the boulders until he reached the bottom of the slope. Then he made his way to the bank and gazed into the water. Suddenly he hissed. "OH NO!" I thought. "What's that cub found now? Not another snake?!"

Well, it turned out that Lucky was startled by his own reflection. He'd never seen it before!

I watched him stick his paw into the water and look puzzled when the strange lion cub vanished. So he sniffed the water and stepped into it, slithering in the slippery mud. Just then his mother called and he scampered back to the others. His fur was wet and straggly and his legs were muddy brown. I tried not to laugh – I felt it was bad manners – but just then he looked more of a "Mucky" than a Lucky.

MUCKY LUCKY

Bignose sniffed angrily at her scruffy cub. Then she crossly licked off the mud with her rough tongue. I guess the lesson of all this is that the world is full of mystery for a young lion cub. And Lucky still has a lot to learn...

LUCKY MEETS HIS PRIDE

March 4

On Monday I got up at 3.30 am to see the lions. Mary said that any day now Bignose would be taking the cubs to meet the rest of the pride and I badly wanted to see what the other lions did. How would they get on with the cubs?

It was another dramatic dawn. I heard the lions roar and the hyenas shriek as I watched the first light gleaming on the big slope and turning the horizon orange.

As it happened, we nearly missed the big event. Mary was having radio-receiver trouble and we couldn't get the signal from Bignose. But James reckoned he could find the lions, and he led me into some bushes. Then he crouched down and showed me some marks in the dirt.

"Look, Mr Leo – lion tracks!" he said. (Don't ask me why Mary and James have started calling me "Mr Leo", I don't know!)

LION TRACKS

Well, I looked down and made out the marks of four toes and a large heavy heel in the dirt. James was right, a lion *had* walked this way.

A few minutes later James came across another clue. He pointed out some scratch marks on a large tree. They had been made by a lion's claws. Cats do the same thing – have you ever seen a cat scratching a

tree or the furniture? Ginger is always ripping chunks out of my sofa. Mrs Matthews once saw Ginger at work and said: "He's sharpening his claws – it's only natural."

But James told me that cats and lions aren't actually sharpening their claws – they're exercising the muscles that control the claws. These muscles have to be strong because lions use them to grip big animals and bring them down.

We were following a narrow track among the bushes when suddenly James dropped down on all fours.

"Look!" he exclaimed. "Lion droppings!"

Well, even I could see they were droppings.

"They smell fresh," said James excitedly. "If they're warm then they're very fresh and the lions are nearby – you have to touch them."

I felt the blood drain from my face. The smell was bad enough.

"Go on, Mr Leo!" laughed James. "You'll be a real lion hunter then!"

So I did. The lion poo felt warm, but I was past caring. I used all the water in my water bottle to try and wash my hand, but it was still smelly. At lunchtime I had to eat my sandwiches one-handed.

I was still trying to wipe my hand when we heard a growl. My mouth went dry as we slowly made our way towards the sound. The lions were sprawled out, like sunbathers on a beach, about 200 metres away! For me, seeing the whole pride together for the first time was a heart-stopping experience. So I took a photo to show you, too!

THE PRIDE - CAN YOU SPOT LUCKY?
HE'S LOOKING AT BIGNOSE

I couldn't take my eyes off the two big lions who rule the pride. I'm calling them Oldie and Baldy. Oldie is the bigger of the two. He would be taller than me if he stood on his hind legs, and he must weigh at least 250 kg – that's a quarter of a tonne! Just imagine him leaping on your bed! He's got a torn ear and his bristly chin hairs look like an old man's beard. Baldy isn't exactly bald, but he's got a bare patch in his mane that could be the site of an old wound.

Besides Bignose, there are two other lionesses. Sorepaw (she walks with a limp) and Gran (Mary says she's the older one. She's got two broken teeth and reminds me of my granny!) We think she's probably the mother of Bignose and Sorepaw because female lions stay together in the same pride.

Sorepaw has two cubs the same age as Lucky and his sisters, and there are two bigger cubs almost two years old called Hungry and Scarface. Hungry's a skinny female, and Scarface is a male with yes, you guessed it, a scar on his nose. Mary said that one of the big males might have scratched him – or he might have got slashed by a thorn bush.

Bignose walked up to Baldy and Oldie, happily rubbing and licking their cheeks in greeting. Lions make scent from special areas on their faces. They rub heads when they meet in order to share this scent – and Ginger does it to me too.

Today Lucky and his sisters played tug of war with twigs. Mary says she's seen the adult lions play this game too – it seems to be a favourite with them all. Lucky was the first to get bored of the game. He went up to Baldy, who was lazing on his back with his big paws stuck in the air. At first Lucky seemed scared of this sleeping giant. Then he started chewing Baldy's mane. Baldy rolled over, lifted his head and growled. That would have scared me off, but Lucky trotted round and sank his little fangs into Baldy's backside!

"Oh-er!" I thought.

Baldy snarled and Lucky scurried off to the safety of his mum.

Has my lion cub got a death wish?

It's easy to think that lions are magnificent and proud and lovely – and so they are. But a lion is a killer creature that can break your arm with a savage swipe of its paw. That snarl said it all.

Mary reckons that Lucky and his sisters are Baldy's cubs. He seems to enjoy playing with them. Oldie is less interested. When Lucky tried to play with him, he thumped the ground with his tail – lions do that when they're feeling cross or grumpy. I bet teachers would beat the ground all the time if they had tails.

Just then, Bignose did something that you won't read about in nice little animal stories – but I'm going to tell you because it happened, and because it's my job to report what really goes on in the wild. She peed on a nearby bush. Then Baldy did something really odd – he sniffed the bush, closed his eyes and looked like he was snarling.

"He's flehmen," said Mary.

"Flaming what?" I asked, trying to be funny. Being a lion enthusiast, I knew what she meant.

"Fleh-men!" smiled Mary. "It's the name for that face he's pulling. He is drawing the scent into his mouth. He has a sensor that tells him if Bignose is ready to mate again."

WHO ARE YOU PULLING FACES AT?

LEO'S LION NOTES
CHEMICAL MESSAGES

1. For a lion, peeing is more than a routine job. It's a chemical calling card telling the other lions what's going on. Males use it to mark the edges of their territory to warn off other lions.

2. Before you get put off lions, I ought to point out that a male cat will do exactly the same thing. Ginger did this on my best curtains a couple of years ago and I never got rid of the smell!

March 11

You might think that living in a pride is a bit like living with a nice cosy little family – but yesterday put things in a different light. I mean, it gave me a shock and showed me what being a lion is really all about.

Lucky and his sisters are now really part of the pride. They know the smells of the other lions, and the sounds they make. The other pride members know them – they're all one big happy lion family. You can tell by the way that the cubs and the other lions look at one another without surprise or fear. So I thought everything was fine ... until I came across the lions having breakfast.

It was another bright sunny morning and already rather hot. We arrived late (the Land Rover had an over-heated radiator). As usual the lionesses had done the hunting, and by the time we'd got there they'd killed a zebra. You could see its stripy body and its hooves sticking stiffly in the air.

Bignose, Gran and Sorepaw were sharing their meal with a cloud of busy buzzing flies. The red raw meat was crawling with flies, but the lionesses weren't bothered. They were used to it. I could hear them crunching the bones and the scraping sound their rough tongues made as they licked the flesh from the bones. It's nice to see someone enjoying their food but I felt the lions could do with a few table manners. It was even more disgusting than dinner duty in the school canteen!

Just then James nudged me and whispered, "Mr Leo, can you see the cubs?"

Well, it was hard because the cubs were so small, but at last I could make them out. I saw that Lucky was about to sneak up and grab a piece of flesh. But before he could get near the meat, Bignose turned on him and snarled until he shrank away to where his sisters were watching hungrily.

BACK OFF, LUCKY!

Now you might think that's unfair. I mean, imagine if your mum kicked you out while she ate and you got her half-chewed scraps! But instinct tells Bignose that she must stay strong to hunt and make milk for the cubs. If she weakens they'll all die. It's a hard lesson, but for lions the eating order is crucial for staying alive.

Suddenly all three lionesses looked up with blood-reddened faces. I could see they were startled because their eyes were wide and dark. And a moment later I saw why. Oldie and Baldy bounded from the long grass to grab their share of the meat — THE LION'S SHARE! The big, strong male lions often do this: they chase the females away and scoff the best meat themselves.

After a bit of snarling and growling, the females slunk off and the males settled down to eat, making happy lion grunting noises. Once again Lucky padded over to join the feast. This is bold behaviour for a cub – Lucky might be the smallest but he's also the bravest. Or maybe he was too hungry to care. I could see his sisters watching in alarm and my heart sank. Eating with a male lion is as dangerous as sticking your head into its mouth!

Food brings out the worst in lions. They turn selfish and greedy and, well, plain nasty. Some lions even kill cubs just for stealing a bite of their food.

I held my breath.

Oldie lifted his head and snarled. But Baldy was in a more generous mood. He edged over to make room for Lucky. Once again my cub has lived up to his name! Soon he was digging his little paws into

LUCKY'S BIG DINNER

the dusty ground as he tore strips of meat from the bones. With timid whimpers his sisters trotted over to try their luck, but Lucky wouldn't move over for them. Maybe he was practising to be a selfish grown-up male lion.

Afterwards Oldie and Baldy lay sprawled in the warm sun. Both lions lay on their backs with their feet in the air and their white chins pointing at the sky. The sight of their big bulging bellies reminded me of the shape of my tummy after my Christmas dinner. And talking about food...

LEO'S LION NOTES
FOOD AND FEEDING

1. Lions have 30 sharp teeth for biting and tearing meat.

2. A male lion needs six kg of meat a day, but can guzzle 50 kg in one huge meal. That's like you or me eating 34 steaks for supper! It might sound greedy, but if you didn't know where your next meal was coming from, you might pig out too.

3. The lion may not eat again for five days or more.

An hour later there wasn't much left of the zebra, but the lionesses were still snarling over the bones and Hungry and Scarface had muscled in to grab the few tattered raggedy bits. A dust crowd of vultures craned their scrawny necks to get at the leftovers. Meanwhile, Lucky and his sisters crunched the smaller bones in a disgusting way.

"The cubs are sharpening their teeth," said Mary. "It's a lion's idea of a toothbrush."

SWISH!
SWISH!

"I think I'd prefer dental floss!" I replied.

Now I don't want to spoil your day, but I think that our lions are in trouble. This morning we heard more roaring than usual and Mary thinks that some young male lions might be moving into the territory and trying to take over the pride. This could spell real danger for Lucky and his sisters. All we can do is wait and see what happens...

March 18

Mary was right about the takeover bid, and I've got a terrible tale to tell. Two days ago two stray young males attacked the pride. I'd better explain first why these young males were so dangerous...

LEO'S LION NOTES
YOUNG MALES AND PRIDE WARS

1. Male lions get kicked out of their pride when they're about two. They haven't learnt to hunt, and as they get bigger it becomes more difficult for the lionesses to feed them. So they go off to try hunting for themselves, or steal meat from hyenas and cheetahs. As ever, staying alive is the aim and there are no rules.

WHAT A CHEATER!

2. But the males have a problem. Their manes start to sprout and it's hard to hunt with a great big scary haircut that can be spotted miles away by any animal they might want to catch.

3. To stay alive, the young males need to take over a pride and force the pride's lionesses to hunt for them.

4. Once they've taken over, the young males kill the cubs. A sharp bite to the back or neck is all that's needed. This may sound really

cruel, but it's the only way to get the lionesses to mate and bring up the new males' cubs before more males come along.

5. You'll be shocked to hear that the lionesses are willing to make friends with the new males and mate with them.

That's the way things are round here. A lion territory is like a little kingdom – always being fought over and changing hands – or should I say "changing paws"? And it's always the strongest lions that win.

I saw the new males last Monday. They both had blond manes and looked so alike I reckoned they were brothers. I knew they were trouble as soon as I set eyes on them – male lions hide if they don't want a fight, but these two were as bold as brass. They looked big and strong and frighteningly fit, like they'd been in a lion gym for a few months. You could see they were itching for a fight.

HERE COMES TROUBLE!

Now I'm no mind-reader but I was certain I knew what was going through Bignose's head. She was watching from a safe distance with her body stiff and her muscles tensed up. She was thinking, "Shall I fight and risk getting hurt? Maybe I should run away and try to save my cubs?!"

Her tail thumped the ground as she weighed up the choices: shall I run and hide? Shall I fight and risk death? Meanwhile Lucky, Orange and Lemon were crying and cowering behind their mum. They were totally terrified. And so was I! As I watched through my binoculars, my sweaty hands shook until I could scarcely see what was happening.

Bignose lowered her head and hissed like an angry cat. It was a warning, but the young males came closer. They were ready to attack.

Suddenly, Oldie and Baldy burst from the bushes. They may have been scared but they didn't show it. First they roared, then they charged. One invader turned and ran off into the long grass and in a flash Baldy was after him. The other lion froze and then bravely ran at Oldie.

Mary says that our lions sometimes fight, but it's a bit like brother and sister squabbles. They tussle but they don't mean any harm and when one wants to give in, it simply rolls on its back. But this was no game. It was the real thing.

The two lions clashed. They were snarling and clawing and wrestling and rolling in a big cloud of dust. I saw Oldie scratch the other lion's muzzle and draw blood.

A BITE TO THE FINISH!

Then it was over. The blond lion tore away and ran. Oldie chased him for a few moments and then stopped and roared as if to say, "AND DON'T COME BACK, YOU SAD LOSER!"

The roar started as a low angry rumble coming from deep inside Oldie's body. Then he lifted up his great head, parted his black lips and opened wide his huge purple mouth. And out came this huge, thundering, heart-stopping, nerve-jangling, earth-shaking storm of sound. It's like nothing else I've heard – I can only describe it as a giant sawing wood – really slowly...

The chase was over. Oldie knew better than to go after his beaten opponent. The enemy lion might turn and fight and do some real damage! Lions aren't cowards – they're just street-wise.

The fight made me realize why male lions have manes: the thick hair protects their necks in a fight. This is bad news for poor Baldy. I touched my bald patch and felt glad that we humans don't fight like lions. Anyway, Lucky is safe ... and I feel really proud of my pride!

Now I want to finish this week's entry by telling you about my daily routine. I'm afraid it's not as exciting as Lucky's life but I've been meaning to write about it for ages. It'll help you imagine what life is like out here...

MY DAY

4 am. Wake up - yawn. It's still dark. Get dressed.

4.30 am. Mix powdered milk and water. Light stove, heat water and make myself a vile-tasting cup of tea. For breakfast I eat cereal that I bought in the camp shop. All in all it's not the worst breakfast I've ever had - but it's nearly the worst!

About 5 am. Mary arrives to pick me up.

All day ... looking for lions, watching lions, etc.

About 6 pm. Mary drops me off. I'm usually shattered, but I try to write my diary while the day's happenings are fresh in my mind.

6.30 pm. Evening meal. A typical meal is vegetable soup or baked beans heated in the tin. I never want to go near instant soup again in my life! Right now I think I'm going to turn into a giant mug of instant soup!

ME!

7 pm. Washing-up is always hard. I use some of the warm water left over from cooking.

7.15 pm. The rest of the warm water is used for washing, shaving and cleaning teeth.

7.30 pm. Make sandwiches for tomorrow. Every week I walk to the Safari Camp and buy bread and all the other stuff I've run out of.

8 pm. Listen to pop songs on Kenyan radio, or read a book by the light of my torch.

Often I find myself gazing up at the bright stars, wondering what will happen to the lions. I wonder what the future holds for Lucky?

HEAT AND HUNTING

March 25

I bet you think I spend all day watching lions.

WRONG! Often we don't spot anything for hours at a time. Maybe we can't get a signal from Bignose's radio collar, or the lions are a long way from a track and hard to find. I haven't been boring you with these dreary details.

The odd thing about the Mara is that although it's alive with wildlife, it often looks empty. You see, the Mara is so big that all you can see is grass and rocks and little round hills, and the odd mound built by little ant-like creatures called termites.

I AIN'T NO ANT!

At present the days are getting hotter and hotter and the grass is drying up, wilting and turning yellowy brown. The whole of the plains are now lion coloured, and this makes the lions harder to spot.

On Monday we were looking for them.

"There's one!" I called to Mary, who was driving.

She stopped the Land Rover and tried to see it. She couldn't.

"There! It is!" I insisted – excitedly jabbing my forefinger in the general direction.

Well, it took ages for us to realize that I was pointing at a boulder. I had been fooled by the shimmering heat. Even I wouldn't be that stupid normally.

SPOT THE DIFFERENCE!

As I said, it's been really hot this week. I must be sweating a bucket of water a day. I'm not sure I can stand this heat much longer – it's hard to think straight. My body feels slow and heavy, my feet are sweaty, my armpits are sticky and my sour-smelling shirt sticks to my prickly back. I can't stop thinking of iced drinks and swimming pools. I wonder if it would be nice to wallow in mud like a hippo?

The heat is bothering the lions too. For one thing it seems to encourage the blood-sucking flies. We found the pride zonked out in the shade of the only tree for miles around, looking as glum as lions can look, with their tails flicking furiously at the tiny pests. If only they could peel off those thick fur coats, you'd be sure that they would. But they can't, so here's what they do instead:

LEO'S LION NOTES
KEEPING COOL

1. Lions don't move much in hot weather, because moving makes them hotter.

2. Heat is tough for lions because, like cats, they only sweat through the pads of their paws. Did you know that when a cat feels scared, it leaves wet paw marks on the ground?

3. Lions pant to lose moisture from their mouths – this takes heat from their bodies. Our lions have been panting like gasping fish in the heat.

SPOT THE COWARDLY LION!

4. They also lose heat from their ears and noses. That's why desert lions have bigger ears and noses than other lions. In fact the cooler blood in their noses stops their brains from overheating!

I wish I had a GIANT-sized nose and ears!

April 1

I've spent most of this week near the water hole. It's like a lion canteen – all the lions do is hang around and wait for dinner to arrive on four legs. At the moment the water hole is half its usual size – the rest is dusty, dried-up mud. But it's the only place for the other animals to get a sip of water, and the lions can pick their moment to attack.

The lions drink too. They take ages while the thirsty zebra stand around miserably flicking the flies with their tails.

HURRY UP!

The lions seem happy to keep them waiting – yesterday I timed Bignose drinking for 11 whole minutes.

The zebra are careful to keep a safe distance and they always stare at the lions with their ears pricked up. Well, I don't blame them for being worried – they know very well that the lions will eat them if they can. This week the lionesses caught a zebra that walked into an ambush they'd set near the water hole. A zebra's life is never safe when there are lions about.

LEO'S LION NOTES
DRINKING LIONS

1. When lions drink, they use their tongues as scoops to spoon up the water. Cats drink in the same way. Give them a saucer of water and watch closely to see how.

SLURP!

2. Lions only drink a little at a time – that's why they're slow drinkers.

3. Lions prefer to drink every day, but if there's no water they can get by on the moisture in meat or juicy plants, and they even eat melons. It's as close to being vegetarian as a lion ever gets!

A disaster happened this afternoon. Lucky, his sisters and the lionesses were dozing near the water hole and there wasn't much happening. Suddenly I spotted something trotting by the water's edge — it was a female warthog.

LEO'S LION NOTES
WARTHOGS

1. A warthog is a kind of burrowing pig. It has a grey-brown body, skinny legs, a mane on the back of its head and nasty-looking tusks. Warthogs get their name because the males have lumps on their faces like giant warts — they wouldn't win any beauty contests!

UGLY WARTHOG!

2. Sometimes a lioness brings back a live warthog to teach her cubs to hunt. It sounds cruel, but have you ever wondered why cats like Ginger bring live mice into the house? Our pets are trying to teach us how to hunt.

I decided to creep closer and take the warthog's picture.

The warthog was wallowing happily in the slippery-sloppy mud. Suddenly she saw me. She scrambled to her feet and was after me! I took one look at her tusks and ran. We dashed twice round the water hole and I was beginning to think that I'd die of a heart attack when I tripped. The world whirled like a sock in a spin-dryer as I fell in the water – SPLOSH!

I found myself on my hands and knees, soaked and covered in mud. There was mud on my glasses, mud in my boots, mud in my ears, and mud up my nose. My face was a mudpack, and I expect I had brown muddy teeth too. Thank goodness my camera was safe in its waterproof case!

I sat down, took off my dirty glasses and spat out a mouthful of muddy Mara water. Then I saw the warthog – she was parked in front of my nose. She thrust her ugly snout up close so I felt her hot sour breath. My heart stopped, well that's how it felt. But all she did was sniff me, wrinkle her snout in disgust and trot away. She must have felt confused when I turned into a mud-monster. Meanwhile Mary was laughing until she couldn't stand up.

Right now it's as dry as the Mara ever gets, and I still managed to get wet! Mary dropped me at the Safari Camp and I mooched grumpily in search of a shower. I was covered in dry mud and looked like the monster from the brown lagoon with two pink patches around my eyes. And that's when I heard a little kid yell, "Look, Mummy, it's a HIPPO!"

IT'S ME, LEO, HONEST!

I turned and discovered I was being filmed by a group of curious tourists.

April 8

I've got an apology to make, but I'll leave it till later. The big news is AT LAST IT'S RAINING! The long rains have come. They started a couple of days after the warthog incident. I was so happy I dashed out of my tent, danced in the downpour and performed a very fine version of "Singing in the Rain".

When it rains around here, it *really* rains. It was like someone had left a shower going full blast. The sky seemed to yawn open, and down poured an amazing amount of water. Oddly enough the drops were MASSIVE – not little spitty-spotty drips like you get at home – but great big sloppy rain splats.

I'm sure some raindrops were three cm across and I should know – I was soaked in seconds!

I was still singing when I saw six tourists in a land cruiser. They were the same group who had seen me covered in mud, and now they were filming me prancing about in the rain!

I'M SINGING IN THE RAIN!

HOW EMBARRASSING! I ducked into my tent and put my head under my pillow. Then I drummed my feet on the bed and tried not to scream too loudly.

After an hour, the person upstairs turned the shower off and the rain stopped. Just like that! The Mara looked lovely. The air felt fresh and clean, and I heard plovers singing. There were flying termites all around me and an adventurous stick

WINGED TERMITE

insect was climbing up the side of my tent. Moths and big yellow swallowtail butterflies fluttered amongst the tall grasses and there was a shiny new

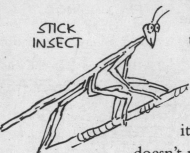
STICK INSECT

rainbow in the clear bright sky. And if you think that sounds pretty, you should have seen it in real life!

Although they call it the "long rains", it doesn't rain all the time. Most of the day is dry and then in the afternoon you see thunder clouds rolling over the escarpment and lightning flickering amongst the clouds. I spent ages watching it on Tuesday – who needs daytime TV when you've got the weather to watch?

BUTTERFLY

Actually, I must have watched it for too long because I strained my neck looking up, and had to go around all evening rubbing it and staring at the sky – this was the only comfortable position I could get into. I felt like some kind of half-crazy astronomer. Anyway, I've been leading up to a bit of a confession: my neck was so sore I've missed seeing the lions this week, er, sorry, readers!

Hopefully I'll be better soon.

April 15

My neck is better and Mary and I have been out lion-watching – but it's really messy work! As the plain gets wetter and puddles appear, I've become the world's greatest expert on MUD.

I've seen every form of mud you can imagine, and a few you wouldn't want to. There's red mud and black mud and gooey mud and gloopy mud. There's smelly mud (with droppings), squelching mud, and squishy, slippery, sloppy mud. But it's all 100% genuine DIRTY MUCK!

As a mud expert I see mud really close and stick my nose into it. Whenever the Land Rover gets stuck, I have to push it out. So far, I've been splattered three times, and fallen face down six times.

FIRST TIME · SECOND TIME · THIRD TIME!

Red mud is hard to drive in, but black mud is worse because it's slimy and sticky. And there's more driving than usual now because the lions have followed the gazelle north to drier ground.

Although the rain is splattering and clattering on the windscreen and the jerky old wipers have a hard job trying to keep it clear, thanks to Bignose's radio collar we usually manage to find the lions easily. But they're always sheltering from the rain. They still get

WET LIONS

wet, but I think they like it. The rain cools them down and they can shake the sopping drops off their coats and manes.

A lion's greasy coat is actually waterproof and that's quite handy in this weather. I could do with one of those myself!

The wet weather has brought out the mosquitoes, and every night they have a party in my tent. Mind you, I can't hear them too well because the cicadas (a kind of noisy grasshopper) make such a din — it's worse than an all-night party next door. Why can't they take a night off and let me have a decent sleep? The only time they take a break is when it rains.

Have you ever listened to the rain? Last night I spent hours doing just that. The tapping on my tent isn't like a drum. It's softer and wetter, and of all the hundreds and thousands of raindrops, no two sound alike. Some are quiet and others loud, some are hard and others soft – so you hear plutt! PLUTT! plitt! PLOTT! And then I felt a cold drip on my nose and realized that my tent had a leak. Take it from me – cold water poured over your face at two am really does get you out of bed fast.

April 22

This week Lucky has been to lion school. Well all right, he and his sisters have been playing hunting games, and this training for the future is as close to going to school as a lion ever gets.

The game begins when one cub does a funny prancing walk, and Mary says this means "let's play!" Like most male cubs, Lucky is now bigger than his sisters and plays rougher – he's definitely not the runt of the litter any more. But the cubs never use their claws for playing – they don't want to risk hurting one another. I wish human kids were that thoughtful!

Hunting is what lions do best. Look at a lion and what do you see?

I see a killing machine with whiskers.

ROBO-LION!

LEO'S LION NOTES
HUNTING

1. A lion's ears turn in several directions to pick up the sound of prey (prey is the animals they hunt). The two ears can even point in different directions if necessary!

2. Lions are great night hunters. They have a shiny layer inside their eyeballs called a tapetum that shows up when you shine a light into their eyes. It reflects extra light into the area of the eyeball that detects light.

3. A lion can pull down a zebra twice its size. A lion's jaws are strong enough to grip around the zebra's throat or over its mouth and nose until it stops breathing. And a lion is strong enough to drag the zebra over 100 metres – you'd need six men for this job.

4. Even a lion's tail is useful in hunting. It helps to balance the lion as it leaps on its prey.

Now is that a killing machine – or what?

April 29

I actually saw a hunt today. It was an experience I'll never forget – every bloodcurdling, bone-crunching, stomach-turning, flesh-tearing moment of it...

Living in a pride makes it possible for a lioness to hunt, even if she has cubs. She leaves her cubs with her sister or mum and off she stalks in search of supper. She's like a busy working mum leaving the kids with their auntie or gran whilst she goes to the office. Mind you, I don't suppose your mum leaps on zebra in the office.

I'M LATE FOR WORK!

It was a sunny morning, but the grass was still soggy after the rain we had last night. (I'm glad I mended that hole in my tent!) I spotted Lucky about 200 metres away. Gran and the cubs were on a low mound in the shade of an acacia tree. Lucky had padded to the edge of the slope, eager to see what was going on. Lions are better at seeing distant objects than we are, and I'm certain that Lucky had a really good view.

Today the lions were hunting gazelle.

"You can see the gazelle are pronking," said Mary.

"Ponging? I can't smell them!" I replied.

Mary laughed. She has a good sense of humour, bless her.

"I said pronking, Mr Leo. It's the jumpy walk gazelle do when they know they're being stalked by a lion."

Well, I felt a bit of a pronker!

Every type of animal has a warning call. For example bushbuck make a kind of barking sound, and baboons go, "WAH-HOO!" Mary made me listen to some twittering birds.

BUSHBUCK

BABOON

FRANCOLIN

"They're francolins," she told me. "They're warning that lions are on the prowl."

Just then I spotted Hungry and Sorepaw creeping through the long wet grass – but I couldn't see Bignose. On its own, a lion has a one in 12 chance of catching anything, but a gang of lions has a one in three chance, so the lionesses always hunt together.

I couldn't see Oldie or Baldy – but that didn't surprise me. The males rarely help. Their manes give them away and Mary says they can't afford to get hurt. They have to stay in peak condition to fight off other males.

Then Hungry made a mistake. She'd been struggling to control her excitement for several minutes. Her tail swung from side to side as she crept through the long grass. She looked like Ginger when he stalks birds. Her thin body shifted uneasily, her strong leg and back muscles knotted up and then ... she charged.

OOPS - TOO SOON!

For a hunting lion, distance is everything. Gazelle gallop at 80 km an hour, but a lion struggles to hit 56 km an hour, and after 100 metres the lion is hot and panting and puffed out. This means that a lion can't catch a gazelle unless it creeps to within charging distance. But the prey know this and always keep a careful eye on the lion. If the lion gets too close, they make a run for it.

You might think that lions are born hunters, but don't forget those hunting games. Most lion hunting skills have to be learnt, and that's why young lions aren't very good at catching prey. I reckon Hungry was on her first hunt, and that's why she got it wrong!

The gazelle ran off with clouds of dust rising around their long legs. A second or two later, Sorepaw broke cover, but she could see that the gazelle were getting away and she skidded to a halt. It looked like the lions had failed – but then I saw a powerful lioness spring from some distant bushes. It was Bignose! All this time she'd been lurking in ambush. What happened next left me breathless and shocked – it was heart-poundingly exciting and sickeningly violent.

Bignose leaped on a speeding gazelle and dragged it down. In a flash, she'd dodged its wildly kicking hooves and clamped her great jaws around its throat. Without air the gazelle didn't stand a chance. Its legs kicked weakly a few times, then they were still. And just then the rest of the pride turned up to feed.

Soon they were happily ripping chunks of flesh from the bones, and Bignose tugged the stringy gazelle guts with her mouth. We watched the lions eat until only a few scattered bones were left of the gazelle. But for the pride, it was just a light snack.

"In a few weeks," said Mary, "there won't be anything left. Jackals and hyenas will clean up what's left of the bones, and ants will eat any bits left lying around."

So every scrap of the gazelle gets used – nothing is wasted. And that's true for everything around here. Even animal droppings have their uses – busy dung beetles roll them into balls, and lay their eggs inside

YUM! YUM!

them. The beetle grubs actually eat the decaying dung for dinner!

No, I wouldn't fancy dung for dinner, either! But then, nature doesn't waste anything – only careless humans throw their rubbish away!

Now I bet you're thinking that lions are cruel hunters. Well, you might have a point…

LEO'S LION NOTES
LIONS AND HUNTING

1. Sorry, readers – but lions aren't nice caring fluffy creatures. Lions hunt and kill whenever they get the chance – even when they're not too hungry. Mind you, so do cats – and you still like cats, don't you?

2. Lions usually kill the old or weak animals that would die fairly soon anyway.

3. Lions are quite fussy about the animals they hunt. They look for animals small enough to pull down but big enough to make a nice square meal. Zebra fit the menu fine but a squitty little creature isn't worth it unless a lion is starving.

Talking about feeding, I don't want to give you the impression that life in the bush is all powdered soup mix. Every week Mr Edwards and his wife invite me for supper at the Safari Camp. But as luck would have it, this evening Mrs Edwards served me a steaming plate of spaghetti and minced beef. The spaghetti reminded me of Bignose pulling at the stringy gazelle guts.

"NO WAY, PAL!" shouted my stomach. Of course I couldn't tell Mrs Edwards why I suddenly didn't feel too hungry.

HUNGRY LIONS AND ANGRY ELEPHANTS

May 6

It's been a hungry week for our pride. You can tell by their tight empty bellies and the bad temper of the two big males. Even Lucky has been tiptoeing around them like a kid who has just had a really bad telling-off.

And here's the problem: our pride are still outside their territory because of the wet weather, and this week they're close to another big pride that lives in this part of the Mara. On Tuesday I saw one of their black-maned males roaring at Bignose. To avoid trouble, our lions have been lying low – even if that means no hunting and no supper.

When a lion is hungry it goes downhill fast. To be honest, lions are an unhealthy bunch at the best of times. Wriggling worms live in their guts and feed off half-digested food, and lions can develop ingrowing toenails. Well, that's what we humans call them. I suppose for lions it's "ingrowing claws". Either way it hurts a lot.

But round here there's no friendly vet to dish out pills and sound advice – the lions are on their own. And that's how lions can get too weak to hunt and starve to death or fall victim to the ever-hungry hyenas. Right now things couldn't be worse for our lions ... so I think I'd better change the subject...

A few weeks ago I wrote to tell my class how I was getting on in Africa. Today I received a reply:

Dear Mr Dennis
We enjoyed reading your letter and hearing about Africa and Lucky the lion cub. It sounds very interesting, but there's one thing we all want to know. How do you manage to have a bath and go to the toilet?
Do write back and tell us!
From your class at Summerhill School

Well, really! This is a serious scientific project and I don't think my bodily functions have anything to do with watching lions! But as I'm sure you're wondering, too, I'd better explain. Recently I've been taking a weekly open-air bath at Mr Edward's house. The rest of the time I get by with a quick wash and OK, I'm a bit smelly. Just be grateful you don't have to sniff me.

Now I don't want to sound ungrateful, but my bath water comes from the river. It's brown with mud and I hate to think what else. After all, hippos live in the water and guess where they go to the toilet?

And while we're on this delicate subject, I should say that I use a bucket and bury my waste first thing in the morning. Well, I *was* asked!

May 13

The lions are still hungry. Their ribs stick out like posts on a fence and their coats look mangy. Mange is caused by itching mites which make the lions scratch themselves, and make open scabby sores in their sides. It makes me shiver just to look at them.

Bignose is so hungry she can't make milk for the cubs. On Tuesday we watched her growling over a

dead zebra with a crowd
of vultures. The zebra had
been dead for a while. It
was so dead we could
smell it and the best meat
had already been eaten.
There were just a few nasty
stringy bits left for

Bignose, but she didn't waste a scrap.

She was desperate.

LEO'S LION NOTES
VULTURES

1. There are around 40,000 vultures that live
on the Mara or the Serengeti plains, and they
eat 12,000 tonnes of dead animals a year.
2. Six types of vulture fly over the Mara, and
if you look at the sky you'll often see them
gathering over a dead animal.

3. Lions and hyenas are keen to grab any meat that's going, so if they see vultures swooping down, they head off to grab a share of the body.

If the lions don't hunt soon I fear the lionesses will leave their cubs to die. Sorepaw seems to be suffering the worst – she's just skin and bone – and it could be a sign of illness. Lucky no longer plays – he just sits there  for hours looking sad. He's too weak even to pester his mum for milk.

Last night I couldn't sleep for worry.

Worry. Worry. Worry.

May 20

Things are looking better this week. Well I say "looking better" but we can't hang out the flags just yet. Last Wednesday, Mary and I found the lions tucking into a dead buffalo. How they found it I don't know – maybe they stole it from the hyenas, but at least it's a nice big bite to eat.

Yesterday I had an accident. Lucky and his sisters had cornered a porcupine and I was quite worried when I saw what was going on.

According to legend, a lion only eats a porcupine when it wants to die. The story goes that the spines kill the lion. Now that's just a silly story. Lions can eat porcupines. But it's tricky and risky – it's like me trying to eat a giant live lobster. I watched Lucky with my heart in my mouth. One jab of those spines could cripple him.

BEWARE–SPINES!

I crept nearer and watched as Lucky tried to stalk the spiky animal. But just as he was getting close, I heard a growl. Bignose was calling the cubs and they left the porcupine and trotted back to their mum. The porcupine took its chance to scuttle away and I breathed again.

I had just taken a great low-level picture and was feeling rather pleased with myself when I felt a pain. It felt like someone was pushing a pin into my leg. Bignose had already spotted the danger and that was why she'd called the cubs. The ground was teeming with ants and they were teeming my way! Some of them were already swarming up my socks.

A soldier-ant army is like a 30-metre-long monster eating everything in its path. But the worst thing is their bites. Once they sink their jaws into your flesh you can't get rid of them. Even

if you pull the ant's body off, the head burrows under your skin leaving a nasty sore. I imagined two million ant bites — and panicked. The first ants had invaded my trousers and their bites stung like fire.

Soldier ants can strip a rat to bare bones in four hours. I didn't fancy life as a skeleton — so I ran.

HELP!

Mary said I should have spotted the ants earlier as she bashed and batted the ants off my backside. I felt sore all afternoon, and when I got back to my tent I inspected my behind using my hand mirror. It was covered in sores, like a bad case of measles, and stung like mad. I needed help now, so I limped painfully to the Safari Camp.

The camp doctor wasn't too pleased to be disturbed off duty. He ordered me to bend over and reached grimly for his sharp, long-handled tweezers. I'll leave the rest to your imagination except to say it hurt twice as much as you think. The best thing about last night is that in 20 years time it will be a very long time ago.

May 27

Great news! The lions are back in their own territory. The rains have eased and the ground is dry enough for the gazelle and other prey animals to move back,

and the lions have followed them. HOORAY! Now they can hunt properly!

The bad news is that Lucky has made an enemy. This week a small herd of elephants has been grazing near the water hole.

Elephants love the rains because it means there will soon be juicy green grass to eat, and herds of them have been appearing from the forest where they feed during the dry season.

Lucky was sniffing one of their piles of dung. Then he rolled in it – looking like a playful kitten rolling on a rug! Well, really – I expect better behaviour from my lion cub!

CAN YOU SPOT LUCKY?

"I think Lucky wants to be a great hunter," said Mary.

"What do you mean?" I asked.

"He's rolling in the dung to mask his scent. Lions, cats and dogs all do it so their prey will not run away. Lucky is a bit young to hunt though."

Lucky didn't seem to think so. He padded out from the bushes and made for the open plain where the elephants could see him. He was actually trying to hunt the elephants!

"They won't like it," said Mary in a worried voice.

"They can't be scared of a lion cub," I laughed.

"It's not that," said Mary tensely. "Lions kill baby elephants and elephants will kill lion cubs..."

YOU WANNA FIGHT?

"So it's some kind of revenge?"

Mary nodded unhappily.

Elephant herds are made up of females, and they're led by the oldest and biggest female. Now this huge leader flapped her big leathery grey ears, lifted her trunk and trumpeted. Bignose ran towards her, trying to distract her, risking her own life to save her cub. But the elephant drove her away from Lucky. Defeated, Bignose dropped her head and ran for her life.

Lucky was on his own now.

I saw the huge elephant circle round, her trunk swinging furiously. I knew she was looking for Lucky. Her legs were like tree trunks and her heavy feet could squash him in a second. I swept the plain with my binoculars but I could see no sign of the cub. As I watched, the angry elephant plodded furiously back to rejoin the herd.

But where was Lucky?

Was he still alive?

A minute later a small head popped out from a warthog's burrow. It was Lucky. He'd been hiding – clever little guy! But by now Bignose had disappeared.

If Lucky couldn't get back to the pride – he was as good as dead. He was far too young to hunt for himself and there was a long queue of creatures ready to finish him off.

In my college days we drew diagrams showing which creatures ate which other creatures. "Food webs" they're called. But out here in the real world things aren't so neat and tidy. Basically, if one meat-eating creature can eat another it will.

I EAT YOU   NO, I EAT YOU

I think I've said hyenas will eat a lion and lions will eat a hyena. Baboons will eat both of them – or be eaten themselves. Crocodiles will eat whatever they can sink their teeth into, and all of them will happily lunch on a lion cub.

We waited and waited ... and waited some more. I hoped against hope that Bignose would come looking for Lucky. Meanwhile Lucky was wandering round in big circles, whimpering. He knew he was alone, he sensed the danger and he was feeling very, very scared. As the shadows lengthened and the light began to dim, Mary said it was getting late and we had to be off. But I kept pleading, "Ten more minutes – pleeeze." At long last, after even I'd given up hope, Bignose came stalking through the long grass.

WHERE HAVE YOU BEEN?

Lucky trotted over to his mum whimpering with joy. They rubbed faces and then she licked him all over. I came over all sentimental and had to blow my nose. All we needed was an orchestra playing stirring music and a little "THE END" sign popping up to round off the drama.

THE BIGGEST FREE LUNCH
IN THE WORLD

June 3

For the lions the worst is over and the best is yet to come. They're still living near the water hole and this week Sorepaw and Bignose brought down a buffalo so all the lions enjoyed a super-sized supper.

The cubs are stronger and healthier than last month, and their coats look sleek and glossy again. Lucky is playing with his sisters once more. He's growing bigger and now he's definitely the leading lion in their games. And things can only get better!

Soon the lions will have the best hunting of the year – Mr Edwards says that the wildebeest are heading towards the Mara. And I'm not talking about a few animals. He says there are hundreds and thousands of wildebeest – perhaps as many as ONE

MILLION. Scientists call this kind of animal journey a "migration". The lions probably call it a "free lunch".

LEO'S LION NOTES
WILDEBEEST MIGRATION

Here's my drawing of a wildebeest. You can see what odd-looking creatures they are:

1. Wildebeest spend their entire lives living in big herds. The baby wildebeest can walk five minutes after they're born so they won't hold the others up.

2. The wildebeest spend half the year in the Serengeti. Then in June, vast herds head for the Mara in search of lush green grass. The wildebeest run 50 km a day, and when they come to a river or lake, they swim across it.

Well, after the rains we've got grass "growing out of our ears" as the old saying goes.

June 10

Last night was the worst night of my life. In fact I'm still shaking! It all began when I decided to take a little walk at dusk. Now this is the one thing that Wildwatch, Mr Edwards and Mary all warned me never to do. There's a risk of getting lost and being attacked by a lion. But in the past few months I've come to feel that this part of the Mara is my home, and home is where you feel safe.

OK, so I was wrong...

I hadn't seen the lions this week because Mary and James have colds. But I was keen to get a picture of a herd of giraffes at sunset, and followed them quite a way – further than I had planned. Sunset is another magical time on the Mara. The shadows lengthen, the air cools and the light turns golden. As the sun set in a dusty red haze, I took my picture and turned for home.

WHAT A LOVELY PHOTO!

But then it hit me: I wasn't sure which way to go. Actually I hadn't got the faintest idea where I was! I had forgotten my map and compass, I couldn't see any landmarks and I was hopelessly, helplessly LOST!

The air grew cold and the sky glittered with stars. But it wasn't the cold that made the hair on my arms stand up — it was goosebumps! It would have been less scary if I'd known less about lions. You don't have to be scared of lions when they roar at night. It's when they're quiet that you need to worry, because that's when they're stalking you. And at that moment the lions were being very, very quiet. Dangerously quiet.

Now I know I've told you that lions don't usually attack humans but it's the "usually" that bothered me. Some lions *do* kill people and I wasn't keen to meet them. I started imagining the school magazine:

Our science teacher, Mr Dennis, has been eaten by a lion. Leo Dennis (39) went to Africa to study lions and got too close to one. The head teacher said: "Mr Dennis was a teacher hero who made the ultimate sacrifice for education, and this is no time to mention his faults like appearing in assembly dressed only in his underpants."

I was so wrapped up in my thoughts, I hadn't been concentrating on where I was going.

"Got to think, got to think," I told myself grimly, and I forced my brain to do just that. Here I was, lost

R.I.P.
Leo Dennis
HE GAVE
HIS ALL TO
THE LIONS

somewhere in Africa, and I was all alone, except for hordes of hungry hyenas and lurking lions looking for a late-night snack.

My brain cells were still ticking. I remembered what Mary had said about how animals make warning calls when there's a lion nearby. But I couldn't even hear a warning squeak. I stopped and listened for any rustle in the grass that could be a lion. Lions normally don't bother to be really quiet until they're just about to charge. I listened until my ears bled, well, almost. But I couldn't hear any lions. I imagined a pair of hungry eyes watching me from cover. A lion is more likely to attack you if you're scared. So I stood up straight and tried to look fearless.

But just then I heard something. My whole body went weak. My legs tottered like a two-year-old toddler. I'd heard something that was BIG AND ALIVE and creeping amongst the bushes. Suddenly I spotted a big yellow cheese floating in the sky...

A big yellow ... what?

Now I *was* seeing things!

No, it was the moon rising! And by its light I saw that the big beast was ... a zebra peacefully munching grass.

I let out a huge sigh of relief. Lions hate moonlight – it makes it easier for prey animals to spot them and they don't often hunt on moonlit nights. The moonlight gleamed on the distant escarpment and now I could see it, I could work out the direction of my tent. I was saved!

Two hours later, with wobbling legs and a weary body, I dragged myself back into my tent. I won't do that again in a hurry. I'll be staying in tonight – that's for certain!

PHEW!
MADE IT!

July 15

In the month since my night-time near-disaster I've been back home. It felt strange sleeping in a bed with sheets on a comfy mattress, with a proper roof over my head. But I'm pleased to say that Ginger is looking happy and well-fed, and not missing me at all. Mrs Matthews says I've lost weight – which pleased me a lot. I also found time to pop into school to tell my pupils about Lucky. But I couldn't stop thinking about Africa – and I'm over the moon to be back.

I'm sitting by the Mara river and watching the greatest, wildest show on Earth. Yes, the wildebeest are here and right now they're trying to cross the river. But it's easier said than done, because the river is still high after the long rains and the coffee-brown water is jumping with crocodiles.

The wildebeest slither down the steep muddy bank and plunge into the water and swim across in a great wave of muscle, hooves and horns. Then they try to scramble up the equally steep and muddy far side. Every so often one of the wildebeest – usually

one of the calves – disappears
into the water and up pops
another contented-looking
crocodile.

Being birds, the
vultures can't smile but
I'm sure they would if they
could. There are enough drowned wildebeest ending
up on the mud banks in the river to give every
vulture on the Mara the lunch time of a lifetime. I
can see a whole gang of them perched in a tree
looking like overfed Victorian undertakers, and I'm
sure they're far too fat to fly.

I've just spotted a lion lurking in the bushes a few
hundred metres away! It looks just like Baldy. But if
it is Baldy, then he's outside his territory. I reckon he's
come to inspect all this free food heading the pride's
way. It's strange that the local lions aren't trying to
chase him away – maybe they're too busy hunting
wildebeest to care.

A few hours later

I watched the wildebeest until sunset. And they were
still coming as the evening light turned the dust from
their hooves into a kind of red mist. There were just
too many wildebeest to count!

July 22

On Monday I met Mary and James. James is on holiday after an elephant wrecked his school. I bet you don't believe me, but these things happen in Kenya. The children were growing vegetables and  one night a hungry elephant got over-excited. James seems sorry not to be at school, bless him. How would you feel if your school was flattened by an elephant? Hey – less of that cheering, please!

On Tuesday, Mary took me to the village to look at the damage. The school is flattened sure enough. It's flatter than a pancake with a tin roof on top. But writing about the day makes me shudder because of my dreadful experience in the toilet. This is embarrassing and it doesn't have anything to do with lions, so I'll tell you about it if you don't tell anyone else – do we have a deal?

I've been suffering a touch of tummy trouble this week. It must have been something I ate and I've had to go to the toilet rather a lot. Anyway, Mary was telling me about the village and how they don't have running water and how the villagers dug a deep pit for their toilet waste ... when my trouble started up again.

Mary showed me a tumbledown shack. "Be careful, Mr Leo," she warned, "black mamba snakes sometimes hide in the hole in the floor. If you see one — you get out of there!"

Black mamba snakes are poisonous, of course, but I was desperate enough to risk anything. In fact I was already running for the toilet door.

The toilet turned out to be a hole no wider than my head above a deep pit that gave off the worst smell on Earth. I was squatting miserably over the hole when I heard something rustle beneath me. I imagined a black mamba snake slithering up to sink its deadly fangs into my bare backside. Peering fearfully into the gloom I saw a movement. Lots of movement. The pit was crawling ... with cockroaches. Thousands of cockroaches, all feeding off rotting human poo.

As I looked away in shock I noticed that the roof was thickly hung with cobwebs. And there descending towards my head was the biggest, blackest spider I'd ever seen. It might have been poisonous — I didn't know — I didn't want to know. I froze as the hairy creature landed on the back of my neck and slowly tiptoed down my back before sliding onto the floor and scuttling into the shadows.

Somehow I escaped. But I knew that no upset tummy – not even a man-eating lion – would get me near that toilet again. And now I know why the people of the village so desperately need clean running water and proper drains.

July 29

At the moment, for the lions every day is like Christmas and everyone's birthday all rolled into one. And it's all because the plains are full of wildebeest as far as the eye can see.

HOW MANY WILDEBEEST CAN YOU SEE?

Every day the lionesses set off to hunt. As they draw near the wildebeest, they slow down. When the wildebeest stare at them they freeze and when the wildebeest look away, the lionesses creep forward a few paces. If they manage to get close enough, they charge. So far they've caught three wildebeest.

I'm pleased to say I've seen Lucky twice this week and he's well, although he's still living dangerously. On Tuesday he trotted boldly after the hunt and acted as if he wanted to join in, until Bignose growled at him and he slunk back to join the other cubs. Sometimes I wonder whether that cub has an atom of common sense in his head. Hunting is dangerous — lions could be trampled by the wildebeest. A zebra's hoof could smash a lion's teeth, and a giraffe could kick a lion to death. Dangerous — huh?

But there's one enemy that's far more lethal to lions. This creature is by far the most deadly hunter on the plains. Can you guess what it is?

FIGHTING FIRES

August 5

It's us — human beings! And this week, while Mary has been working on a research project in another part of the Mara, I've been reading a book all about human hunters. It's by Colonel Blatherton Fartpants (or some such name) — and it's called *Lions I Have Bagged!*

Lions I Have Bagged! is full of horrible stories of shooting lions with a high-powered rifle, which the Colonel thought was "jolly ripping fun". But the Colonel's book has got me thinking about lions and people.

LEO'S LION NOTES
LIONS AND PEOPLE

1. Match a human against a wild animal and we are rather pathetic. Even the fastest human runners can just about reach 36 km per hour, which is nothing compared to a lion. But we've got guns and bullets and traps to fight the lions' teeth and claws.

2. Lions lived in Africa, India, the Middle East and even Europe 15,000 years ago. But 2,000 years ago, there were no lions left in Europe, and by the 1900s the last lion had been killed in the Middle East. Now the only wild lions outside Africa are a few skulking in the Gir Forest in India.

In parts of Africa, lions are still being shot by farmers trying to protect their cattle. I'm sure the best way to protect lions is to protect places like the Masai Mara where they can live safely! Sorry to make a speech, readers, but I feel really strongly about saving lions.

August 12

I suppose, like children, lions have to grow up one day, and Lucky's definitely growing up. I saw the pride on Monday and Wednesday and I was amazed at how big he is now. Lucky and his sisters are still fed by Bignose, but already they're looking more like grown-up lions. They don't play as much they did, which is a great pity as I enjoyed watching them.

LUCKY'S GROWING UP!

I've been keeping a low profile for the last couple of days after I had a row with some tourists. Mary and I were watching the pride, and the tourists drove up to the lions in a shiny new land cruiser. They were yelling and honking their horn, and I could see that the lions were upset. The tourists wanted close-up photos. They were like old-time hunters in search of souvenirs – something to show the folks back home. They weren't really interested in our lions.

Mary says these things happen quite often but it made me mad. I felt like picking up some rocks and chucking them at their grinning faces. I didn't go that far, but I did have to say sorry for certain rude words I'd used.

August 19

Right now I'm feeling like blubbing my eyes out. I'll explain why in a moment but I'm afraid I've got some very bad news to tell you.

The wildebeest have been here a while and you can tell. The Mara's looking as chewed up as a school playing field at the end of term. The lions aren't too happy because they hunt better when the grass is longer – it makes it easier for them to sneak up on their prey.

OI, STOP MESSING UP THE GRASS!

So the lions are feeling hungry this week. Once more Lucky is listless. He's taken to padding round in circles and pestering his mother for milk, but I saw her flick him away with her paw. The other lions are in bad shape too – I even spotted Sorepaw stalking a warthog, which she wouldn't do if she had the choice. I hope it was the warthog that chased me into the water hole a few weeks ago.

But the lions' hunger isn't the bad news...

I'll try to explain things as calmly as I can, but inside I feel cross enough to chew the carpet. It all started when I went out with the anti-poaching patrol. And despite what happened, I'm glad George, the patrol leader, agreed to take me. Basically, George and his men are the good guys.

THE GOOD GUYS

As we trundled across the plain in the patrol's Land Rover I wondered what to expect. Everyone except me carried a gun, and the men told me hair-raising stories of shoot-outs with poachers. I felt alarmed as I clutched my night glasses and anxiously scanned the shadows for any sign of trouble.

Seeing in the dark is an eye-opener! I didn't see any poachers, I'm pleased to say – but I did see a group of hyenas tearing at a dead gazelle. The hyenas looked like a cross between a bear and a dog, with sharp jagged teeth and glittering eyes.

LEO'S LION NOTES
POACHING

1. Nowadays, hunting wild animals is banned in the Mara but at night, gangs of poachers try to shoot elephants and rhinos for their tusks and horns. In the 1980s poachers wiped

out two thirds of Kenya's elephants and nearly all the rhinos.

2. Elephant tusk ivory is smuggled to Japan and Hong Kong to be carved into ornaments and rhino horns are made into dagger handles in the Middle East.

3. Like other African countries, the Kenyan Government has set up anti-poaching patrols. It's a tough job – the Mara is a massive area to patrol and the poachers carry guns.

Then we caught sight of a rhino and her baby. The rhino blinked at our light in the bad-tempered short-sighted way rhinos do and then lumbered away with her baby trotting behind.

I was thrilled, but then George said something that horrified me: "They're OK. That's the main thing. But we know there are lions living around here. They will have to be tranquillized and moved to protect the baby rhino."

VERY RARE BABY RHINO

I sucked in my breath and thought hard.

There's a risk that the drugs used to knock the lions out for the move could harm them, and I know that lions can starve if they get moved  from their territory. But rhinos are so rare that I found myself nodding gravely. Until it hit me – I realized George was talking about *our lions*!

I can't describe the feeling of horror – I felt like my stomach had dropped 24 floors in a lift.

"Look," I said crossly, "lions don't attack rhinos. They're not that stupid. They're scared of the rhino's size and its horn."

"Yes, Mr Dennis," said George, "we know that, but the lions will attack the baby rhino. We can't allow it."

Well, we got into one of those endless arguments that goes round in circles and left both of us in a bad temper. But the outcome is clear: unless the park bosses change their minds, next week our lions will be moved. They could be hurt or starve. And in their new home Lucky could be killed by males from a rival pride.

I'm feeling upset just now so I'm not going to write any more. Tomorrow I'll have to write to Wildwatch and tell them the bad news.

August 26

A lot has happened this week, but rather than say how it turned out, I'd better tell you the whole story.

The first person I talked to about it was Mr Edwards. He was sympathetic – he knew what the lions meant to me. He said he'd have to warn the tourists at the camp to stay away from the rhino, and I asked if I could tell them what was going on. Before I knew it, I was making a speech...

I told the tourists how I had come to Africa to keep a diary about a lion. I told them how I had first seen Lucky as a tiny cub and how I had followed his adventures and all the dangers he had faced. Then I said that Lucky and his family would lose their home, maybe even their lives, simply because they were in the wrong place.

TOTTER! CREAK!

As soon as I'd finished I was mobbed by tourists all begging to sign a petition to stop the move. I knew I felt really strongly, but I didn't realize I had it in me to start a protest. Mr Edwards helped to write the petition, and everyone signed it – and that was just the beginning.

The lions have two more special friends: Mary and James. They were shocked when I told them. James cried because he loves lions, and Mary cares about the lions too, and she knows the move could mess up her research.

The petition grew larger and larger. Mr and Mrs Edwards signed. Mary and James signed. All Mary's scientist friends from Nairobi signed and so did James's teacher and all the children and parents from James's school. Hundreds of people have signed the petition – it's amazing that so many people should care about a few lions.

This morning I got the news. Mr Edwards drove over to tell me in person. It seems the Mara bosses are worried about bad publicity that might harm the tourist trade.

Then Mr Edwards told me their decision...

It's only just sinking in – WE'VE WON! WE'VE WON! WE'VE WON! WE'VE WON! After Mr Edwards left I sat on my bed with tears of joy rolling down my cheeks.

The park authorities have agreed not to move the lions unless they actually attack the baby rhino! It's a lifeline for Lucky. George says he doesn't want to move the lions, he only wants to protect the baby rhino. I've given him my night glasses as a "thank you".

And the lions haven't been near the baby rhino this week. In fact they've been hanging out at the other end of their territory hunting zebra. They caught one on Wednesday and Lucky ate with the big males, so he got more than his fair share.

September 2

OUCH! I'm writing this in pain. The grim-faced camp doctor ("Dr Death", I call him) has bandaged my bottom. He seems to think the injuries are all my fault. And despite the fact that Dr Death injected my backside with painkillers, I'm still suffering. Right now I'm too sore to sit down and I'm kneeling on the

A-A-R-G-H!

dusty ground to write this.

As you may have guessed, I've suffered another accident. Well, it was quite a BIG ACCIDENT, actually. It happened yesterday.

At this time of year, Masai farmers set fire to grasslands next to the Mara, and you can see big clouds of dark smoke rolling up on the horizon. It's a good way of getting rid of the tough grass their cattle won't touch, and gives the right type of grass a chance to grow. But some fires spread to the Mara. This was one of those.

Mary and I were watching the lions — not that they were doing much, just dozing in the shade. Lucky, Orange and Lemon were nuzzling Bignose to wake her up and feed them. Suddenly I saw a puff of smoke in the long dry grass 100 metres away.

FIRE!

"It's a fire starting!" said Mary in a hushed voice. "This could be very dangerous."

I'd never seen her so scared – her eyes were wide with fear. Already the smoke was billowing into an ugly great volcano. The grass was as dry as old bones – you could see that it would burn fast. Very, very fast.

"We've got to put it out!" I said.

"It's better if we get out of here," said Mary, making ready to leave.

Looking back I'm not too sure why I did what I did. It might have been to save the lions, although they could have got away. Maybe I was trying to stop the Mara going up in flames.

As luck would have it, I was next to a bush and just by my hand was a straight branch that looked like an ideal fire-beater, so I broke it off. Then, clutching the branch, I charged off towards the fire before Mary could stop me.

"MR LEO – COME BACK HERE!" she screamed.

From close up, the fire looked larger, and more dangerous. It had got fiercer in the few seconds it took me to reach it. Now there were nasty red flames and a crackling noise and a wave of heat that hit me like a giant's oven. I realized that Mary was right, but I was still set on fighting the fire.

"Take that, you stupid fire!" I yelled as I beat the smouldering ground.

At first I fanned the blaze more than beating it out, but then I began to win.

"TAKE THAT, YOU STUPID FIRE!" I shouted again, coughing and spluttering in the stinging smoke. My eyes were streaming with tears and I could scarcely see, but soon there was nothing but blackened grass and smoke and a nasty smell of burning. Too late I realized that the nasty smell of burning was my shorts. My backside was on fire!

The worst moment in the world is when you smell burning and find out it's your bum! The pain is bad, but the terror is worse. I did the right thing – rubbing my rear end in the dirt until the flames went out, but the damage was done – there are painful burns on my backside. Dr Death says I may need hospital treatment and this could be the end of my time in Africa.

14 September

After a few days the pain was easing but I had to fly home to get my burns looked at. The nurses at my local hospital were impressed when I told them how

I'd come to be injured. The news soon spread and the local paper took a picture of me proudly holding up my scorched shorts.

LOCAL TEACHER IS BLAZE HERO!

I've heard that the teachers at Summerhill are calling me "the man with the flame-proof bum".

And I never thought I'd ever be a hero!

My class came to visit me in hospital. They ate all the bananas they brought me, but I didn't mind. I don't like bananas – and it's the thought that counts. It wasn't my fault the nurse skidded on that skin. I felt a right banana when she told me off!

Last night I did a talk at school for parents and pupils and showed them my photos. I'd been looking forward to being the hero of the hour and at first everything went so well. The audience listened open mouthed to my tales of living in a tent and spying on lions. At last I had wiped away the shame of appearing in this very hall dressed only in my underpants.

Just then I knocked over my water, tripped over the table leg and got tangled up in the power lead of the projector I was using to show the pictures. Somehow I landed on my still-sore behind with my feet kicking in the air. And of course someone had to take my picture!

MY MOMENT OF GLORY!

This morning I've been sitting with a big purring Ginger on my lap reading a letter from Mary and James. The fire proved to be what people call "a blessing in disguise" because the risk of more fires made the park wardens move the rhinos away from the lions. So something good came out of it all. And Lucky is safe – that's the main thing!

SO LONG, LUCKY!

21 September

Living in Africa has been the biggest thrill of my life. I've seen things that I couldn't even have imagined back home. I just can't believe it's been eight months – the time has zipped by faster than a leaping lion. There have been good things and bad things, but the biggest surprise was how much I ended up caring about my lion cub.

And that's why I had to see Lucky one more time before I left. But where was he? Mary and I searched all the usual places, but he wasn't there. He wasn't with the other lions or by the water hole or on the rocks. My poor backside felt on fire again from bouncing about in the Land Rover, but I wouldn't give up.

It was dusk by the time we found Lucky. The sun looked like a sizzling red-hot tomato and the horizon was swept by waves of deep crimson. Sunset is a special time for lions. As the air cools and the shadows merge and deepen, they stir from their afternoon snooze, yawn and stretch, and sniff the air. Then they start to pad about, waiting for the darkness and the night's hunting.

Lucky was crouching in the bushes watching the world go by. Just before the sun disappeared he stood up. He enjoyed a long lazy stretch before slipping into the evening shadows like a graceful ghost. If only you could have seen him!

I whispered "goodbye", but of course Lucky didn't answer. He'd been eating well for the last few days and he looked smart and sleek and strong. He's not yet fully grown, and he hasn't got a mane, but he looks big enough to bring down a gazelle. The days when he was "the runt of the litter" are long gone and in a year he'll be old enough to live by himself.

Lions live their lives on the edge. At Lucky's age they get killed in fights or die of disease and hunger, and in Africa no animal gets a second chance. But if any lion deserves to make it, Lucky does — and I really, really hope he will.